William Adolphus Clark

Intellectual people

William Adolphus Clark

Intellectual people

ISBN/EAN: 9783743332973

Manufactured in Europe, USA, Canada, Australia, Japa

Cover: Foto ©Andreas Hilbeck / pixelio.de

Manufactured and distributed by brebook publishing software
(www.brebook.com)

William Adolphus Clark

Intellectual people

INTELLECTUAL PEOPLE.

"Ye swell as though ye had conceived some great matter;
but, as for that which ye are delivered of, who knoweth it
not?" — JOB.

CULTURE.

My theme is culture, and the cultured mind,

Which looks with pity on the common hind ;

Assumes the air of Fortune's favored ones,

And through this life with self-assertion runs ;

Be mine the task, however sad to do,

To bring my subject clearly to the view ;

Ignoring Fear and all its trembling train,

As I go through the classic and the vain.

From early life I 've loved to think how pure,

The mountain streams which " to old Ocean pour ; "

I 've loved to look upon the crystal clear,

On beauty's cheek to note the beamy tear ;

I 've loved to gaze upon the moon's bright face,

As she her course pursues through vaulted space ;

I 've loved in stillness, through the breathless night,

To watch the planets in their steady flight ;

I 've loved to look upon the flaky snow ;

Upon the babe's soft eyes, its stainless brow ;

I 've loved amid the forests oft to roam ;

I 've loved, at sea, to watch its sparkling foam ;

I 've loved to note the dolphins at their play ;

The twilight fade at morn and eve away ;

And on the land, amid its fruitful fields,

To view its charms, and all which harvest yields.

And why? because delicious is the sense

Of gentle truth and sweetest innocence.

I 've loved to think that man might be as pure,

Through culture's care, and learning's varied store;

But years have swept the fond conceit away,

I see that Virtue 's something as a play!

I see that goodness dwells alike with *all*,

That it's a part of both the great and small;

That none are better than they ought to be,

Or love too well, O Christ, to follow Thee!

Then, come sweet spirit of the art of song,

Whose home is where there *never can be wrong*,

Assist my strain and aid me to portray,

How vice in *culture* holds too often sway;

Make clear my mind to see the human soul,

In all its subtle working for control;

Give me the courage to lay bare the ways

" The classic " take in their wild *rush for praise;*

Then shall I show unto my fellow man,

That life is *mean,* though based on culture's plan.

When from the womb the infant moves to light,

To grow in strength for either wrong or right,

Came it among a race of beings *true,*

Culture would prompt it nothing *vile to do;*

But as it grows to think, to act a part,

It gathers knowledge, and corrupts the heart;

While in that brain is stored vast sums of lore, .

In morals, manners, is the creature poor;

'T is taught the classics, natural laws acquire,

Ethics engages, but with less desire;

Religion does, perhaps, excite some **glow**

Of curiosity its truths to know,

Yet, so much else there is the pride to please,

Religion's courted only at their ease.

'T is Culture's *policy* to wing the wit,

To scale ambition's lofty minaret!

To worship only at the shrine of pride,

To shrewdly float on Knowledge's sunny tide.

The *moral sense*, though trained the *right* to hold

In schools and colleges, itself will fold

In close retirement, when the mind may be

Planning and working, *vanity*, for thee!

The sacred rights of others are laid low;

Learning makes possible, *directs the blow!*

For it will do far meaner acts than those,

Who little else than honest impulse knows;

That force which " common things " ennobles more,

Than all a Bacon's genius with his lore.

Yes, honest impulse ! that is much your need,

Ye *cultured swindlers* of every breed ;

If ye have learned all languages to speak,

Have gone through Science, and through Latin,
    Greek,

As Pascal, learned all — all there is to know,

But not as Pascal, bowed in solemn woe ! —

What boots your knowledge if you love to lie,

To cozen ignorance and laws defy ! —

If teems your brain with polished vice, to grind

Whoever meets with your " accomplished mind " ;

If for a debt you owe you 'll slay by art,

Reduce through *chemistry* the human part,

Then to the wave consign the mellow mass,

Concealment seeking for the crime — alas ! —

What boots, I say, your culture, if your deeds

Keep *morals* weeping — ever in its weeds.

Yet, so it does, in cases not a few —

Scholastic rascals ever are in view !

When in the bookstores, they will steal so sly

None can detect them but an expert eye ;

So, too, they 'll steal a brother author's brains,

To lard their writings and increase their gains.

No thieves are there so mean as such who teach

What 's well to practise, and what 's well to preach ;

Oft will their efforts stir the studious crowd

To flattering praise, and plaudits long and loud ;

Yet, will they *sin as serves to deck their wit ;*

Lie right and left, where lying seems to fit ;

They grow in *grace* no faster than may suit

Ambition's ends, *and all its vain pursuits!*

Ye sons of knowledge, and ye daughters, too,

This may I say in perfect truth of you.

Ah, well, what of it, since 't is right to be

Guided by conscience, which is ever free ;

Free to contract, and then expand by turns,

As matters go, and *classic* daily learns ;

For who, oh, *who* can live by *truth alone,*

Or kiss the hand that *throws to it a bone ;*

Who, *human,* can his cultured head recline,

And feel the bread he eats is bread divine?

Do they not know "of intellect complete,"

The *dirtiest morals get for them their meat?*

Do they not know that classes they despise

Are far more honest, though perhaps less wise?

They speak not Greek, nor Newton's Princepts ken,

Not cultured women they, nor cultured men;

They cannot split the glorious right in two,

By polished sophistry, as oft will you;

Their minds untutored in the ways of lore,

Are barren deemed, and, as their pockets, poor;

Yet, many have an honest love of truth,

You 've somewhat slighted from your early youth.

As to your brain, from year to year has crept

The learning which, alone, can make adept,

In all those paths *where figures go one way,*

And that as culture, right or wrong, may say,

The *cause of truth* has gradual ceased to be,

Naught but a plaything, classic, unto thee!

I know not, I, why thus should run to seed

The moral sense, as more the mind we feed;

Yet, *so it is;* the knavish mostly now,

Bear polished intellect upon their brow;

Stupendous frauds, stupendous crimes abound,

Too oft with those where cultured grace is found!

The *petty* thieves, the *petty* vile are those,

Linked but to poverty and all its woes;

Who are imprisoned, while the *genteel knave,*

Oft with success will judge and jury brave.

Crime seems to lose its dark and hideous face,

When *classic minds* may wear it in Life's race.

That this is so, e'en they who run may read;

Culture to culture's aid will surely speed!

Thus have we doved-tailed, wits in specious wrong,

Borne by the force of *sympathy* along;

Living as best they may on doubtful law,

Their conscience worth not e'en a wisp of straw.

Ah, well, what of it, pray; is it not fair

That *intellectual worth* should have our care?

Be treated kindly, though in most things mean,

So rarely just, *preferring the unclean!*

But I could never see why Culture's grace,

Should from her seat sweet justice e'er displace;

No less is crime, because the culprit's brain,

Sparkles with knowledge, either sound or vain.

I'd to the *hempen* give whoever kills,

To prison send who deeds felonious wills;

Nor would I care how *learned* the felon caught,

The more he *knew* would sterner make my thought.

Culture should crimes reduce and not increase,

Should give society e'en greater peace;

In place of which, there is a constant dread

Of startling outrage from the poorly fed;

None feel *secure*, and those *au fait* at life,

Most fear the passions of its active strife.

Religion but a partial check supplies ;

Accomplished rogues " put through " what they
    devise ;

And see no punishment for *them* but law

Our courts administer — too oft but straw —

A dubious slippery thing, the wisest say,

Damning more justice in its beaten way

Than e'er was saved, with all its fervid glow

Of classic lore, and ermine white as snow.

What then are *courts*, if culture does not arm

The judge with conscience, his abiding charm?

They are the *slaughter-houses of the weak ;*

Where *wrong* and *power* dare 'gainst right to speak,

And speak successfully by subtle art,

Which there appears, to do its hireling part ;

To gain a case, perhaps, which they should not,

Were justice better loved and ne'er forgot.

Lawyers will work for what they call a *fee*,

While " strictly right" is hard for them to see ;

Their heartless arguments, on culture based,

Too often are by *legal genius* graced ;

They 'll skin the client and they 'll blind the court ;

Their wit, like other things, is easy bought ;

If goes the case against them, let it go ;

What cares the counsel for his client's woe ;

His pay 's in hand ! e'er long he may appear

Against that client, to renew the tear !

These are our friends at law ; that cultured band

Of sharp logicians, who but take our hand

To take our purse, and often lose our rights,

Heedless who suffers, whom their culture blights !

Of all the mean, the dirty ways of life,

None can exceed the bar's accursed strife;

Where far too many, " sound in legal lore,"

In generous action are supremely poor.

Once in a while a case is fairly tried;

The rules which govern squarely are applied;

But most who litigate to get their dues,

More than one half of what they claim will lose!

These *noble* classics, these high cultured minds,

Against society their wit combines;

And that which should to all a shield be found,

By wit is broken, trampled to the ground!

The law, which every one should highly prize,

The greater part have reason to despise!

Their rights uncertain are, they see it so,

And look on courts as sources foul of woe;

They see false culture there, perverted wit,

And meanness, often, where should honor sit;

They know the longest purse will win the cause;

And sneering say — " such, *such*, are human laws."

Oh, is it strange when intellect delights,

To make a chaos of dear human rights,

And jurisprudence, science so divine!

To gross absurdities and rules incline,

That those " unlearned in law," but loving truth,

Brand law *satanic* and the bane of youth?

Cursing the culture which makes little *clear*,

While burdening life with many a bitter tear —

Oh, is it strange that *sometimes* they will feel,

The sense of outrage to their bosoms steal,

As see they learning with the devil leagued,

Unto the false with eager footsteps speed;

Through which our world is made a fervent hell,

Where Virtue sighs to think it here must dwell?

That this is so, the dullest may observe ;

Culture does not the *cause of honor serve ;*

" Well, granted that 't is thus," Atrides says,

Who aims to figure in false culture's ways ;

" What if the right and wrong *are* somewhat mixed,

What if in law there 's much which can't be fixed ?

Contention ever was the life of man,

Make it ought else, O virtue, if you can ;

The greatest pleasure, contradiction gives ;

It is the zest, main spring of human lives ;

What, would you have a *calm* from day to day,

And wear your life so stupidly away ?

What, would you have the law so *very* plain,

You 've but to state your case and score your gain ?

Methinks, 't is better, as we have it *now;*

That none with certainty the Law should know.

Right 's but a shadow, justice but a dream,

Law is the plaything of a wit supreme ;

What 's *low* must suffer, that the *high* may be

Admired the more as, Genius, born of thee!

We lawyers like uncertainty, 't will drive

The legal mind to study, and to thrive ;

That is the source from whence our riches flow,

That is the practice of the law, you know."

So spoke Atrides with a bloated pride ;

Ready, at all times he, for either side.

A manly practice this, I must confess,

Which mostly thrives where man 's in *most distress!*

Such facts made *Godwin* wish no bar might be,

To foster wrong, while, Justice, pledged to thee !

Such facts as *these* made Bentham mourn the curse

Of that *black art* which aims to make the worse

Appear the better reason in the case —

To win, by *jockeying*, the legal race !

Such facts as *these* do other minds compell,

To own that *law epitomizes hell!*

Whoever has its study dared essay,

Will think it but a comi-tragic play ;

A bat and ball where life is knocked about,

And men are strangely counted in and out.

These cultured minds, so trained to split a hair,

Split human hearts, unheeding their despair ;

Though high their rank, their lives are often *low*,

Less worthy they, the more, perchance, they know

On knowledge grounded, they are seen to wait

With *legal webs*, to snare some trustful pate.

With mind well skilled in *taking* in these flies,

They are, in keeping them, well skilled, likewise;

They 'll eat the oyster while the shell they give

To those who in their wicked art believe;

A precious set to guard *the rights of man;*

Find me a baser, Atrides, if you can.

My heart is saddened with a sense of pain,

To see the cultured crowds so proud and vain;

Vain in the thought *one little head* can hold,

All it may study of our little world;

See where a cheat may be successful done;

Measure the earth and distance to the sun;

Follow the lead of Blackstone and of Coke,

Whose thin distinctions much of mirth provoke;

Giving to custom such an airy turn,

That right, like smoke, doth ever seem infirm;

Gazing with Newton on the vast unknown,

Whilst thinking *cutely* of the things their own :

In part perceiving what there is of life ;

And what will lead directly on to strife ;

Knowing of nature but in small degree ;

Too weak her subtleties to *clearly* see ;

Vain of the nothingness of meat and drink,

While proud to haughtiness of truths they think ;

Which follies move one's common sense to cry,

Ye cultured *nincompoops*, O, haste to die ;

The world, without you, might not be so wise,

Nor near so wicked, nor so packed with lies ;

If ye won't stand *to manly honor fast,*

The world 's the gainer when your days have past ;

No tear should fall when you are laid to rest,

Of all things pestilent the vilest pest ;

For ye have reason plumed to wing its way,

Where craft and cunning hold triumphant sway;

In this yourself disgraced, dishonored God,

Loathed when beneath, as when above the sod.

Some of your number, I may say with pride,

Will not, as Bacon, take a tempting bribe;

Or let a friend be hustled to the block,

When friendship could his prison doors unlock.

There are, thank heaven, 'mong the learned some minds,

Which honest heart and polished wit combines;

Harvard, Marshall, Prescott — they are names,

Which, *trumpet tongued*, this happy truth proclaims.

But such are as the stars which shine through skies,

Where heavy clouds oft shade them from our eyes;

Those clouds of sorrow, born of passions mean,

'Mid "cultured classes" far too frequent seen.

Where 'er we turn, whatever land we see,

There knowledge seems with vice in love to be;

The wit of man and of the *woman*, too,

Will more of *mischief* than good service do!

Only, as God his spirit to the heart,

Through *faith* and *prayer* may graciously impart,

Can Learning's graces lead us on to act,

Justly by all, in honor's rules exact.

Ne'er could I see why Culture's force should sway

The strong or weak from Conscience's beaten way;

Yet, in some graceless, godless wit, behold

A power which does this, crafty, bad and bold;

And as he pleads with cunning art a cause,

Laughs in his sleeve at jury, judge, and laws!

If any doubt a scoundrel at the bar

May grow to be a bright and mighty star,

And ride rough-shod o'er who shall *then* presume,

To soil or pluck his waving, gaudy plume,

To call him rightly by his name, a knave,

Learned though he be, and amiable, and brave, —

If any doubt this, I their pardon crave

When I proclaim them *innocents*, indeed,

Who *very much* a guardian's vigils need.

To me, the *learned*, who mould the times, seem wise

Mostly and only in their own fair eyes.

Yet, if they could and would see how it is, —

The error rampant and the lives amiss,

They might, perhaps, in pity at the sight,

Resolve to shape things somewhat more aright.

They have the power — if they had the will —

All they affect, in righteous ways to drill.

The masses look to *Culture* for their cue;

And, as they get it, wrong or right will do:

If they perceive who lead in life, as *wise*,

All training but the *sensual* despise,

By which the base, the grosser passions thrive,

And from the soul all higher thinking drive, —

If they are made to feel a tender heart,

Which pities suffering and takes its part;

Does what is possible in Christ's dear name

To honor Him, and put who sneer, to shame, —

If they suspect the *cultured* smile to see,

To whom they bend, in love and awe, the knee;

And in whose name they offer prayer to God.

Who will through *Christ* redeem them from the

    sod, —

If they conceive this worship all a *farce*,

And both the covenants of *law* and *grace*,

A sheer invention of the priests to gain

Over the masses a despotic reign, —

What will they do, but quickly turn to those,

Who, " greatly learned," the Christ *divine* oppose:

They will not think *that* can be *really* true

The " finest scholars riddle through and through,"

As they believe; while Scripture laughs to scorn

These puny critics of vain learning born! —

Who beat their brains against its deathless page,

Thinking to shatter *by their truth's great rage*

The precious lore our Scripture doth reveal, —

The Christian's love, his happiness, his zeal!

But though these critics, apt at vain dispute,

Succeed in winning whom their wit may suit,

Yet, *all unshaken* stands God's Word to-day,

As first from sacred pens, it made its way;

A light and comfort to, who hold it dear

Beyond all else — how wise, exact, sincere.

Science can tell us of the road to wealth

And fame — can help us get and keep our health;

Can well acquaint us with the laws which reign,

Through, what of Nature, we may chance attain;

But *short* the distance we can go *that way;*

At second causes we are *forced* to stay.

And when the whole of what is known to be

" Truth *proved* beyond a doubt, as all may see,"

Is massed as *evidence* of Reason's might —

To that *unknown* compared, how mean a sight!

What cause for boasting *this*, of wit of man,

When *all he knows* we closely, careful scan;

When, what he *proves*, alas! is nothing more

Than as *one* pebble to the ocean's shore!

Yet will this pigmy, this *inflated mite*,

So short of reason and so poor of sight,

Set up a cry of fraud against a plan

God has designed to bless conceited man —

A Word Revealed of such *unnatural* cast,

(Unmatched by writings of the present, past)

That *human* wit, unaided by *divine*,

Would not have wrought in this so *misty* line.

It would have worked according to *its way*,

Nor taught of *truth*, fair Nature gives no ray! —

But this doth *Scripture;* yet bears *proof* that He

Who made all things made *this*, O Man, for thee, —

This precious Word, without which who can *know*

The *wrong* from *right* — said not the wisest so?

Said not the sage by whom was Plato taught,

God must himself make certain moral thought,

By word revealed in some decisive way,

Else, would the mind no standard fixed obey —

Else, would the mind, confused by self-conceit,

In no one Master ever *deign* to meet ;

But *many* schools would varied *notions* teach,

And wrong as right would not infrequent preach.

Yes. *needful* as this precious Word Divine

Is thus confessed to be, yet " wits sublime "

In these last days incessantly declare

" Science is all for which we need to care ;

That Scripture, or the so-called Word of God,

Has had its day ! — should rest beneath the sod

Buried from sight, no more to curse mankind

With cruel wars and superstitious mind :

Reason, informed by what may *now* be known,

Is all the God that human wit should own.

If *it* shall fail us, there's no other power

We can avail of any day or hour.

The *Force* creating earth and all we see,

Has no more care for man than for a bee,

Or flower, or any other living thing —

To Reason only may we trust and cling.

All prayers to *it* shall answered be,

If clear the answer, wit, perchance, may see:

All other gods are nought and cannot hear;

Nor know, nor care, for either smile or tear.

We live and die no wiser than the dog;

If aught's beyond, it is a dismal fog.

The soul's a *myth*, the supernatural, sham!

Sin never could, or will, or ought to *damn;*

But, if there *is* a soul, which liveth on,

'T will have a body, with itself as one :

We need not care about that future, *now ;*

Of this life only do we really *know.*"

So prates " great Learning ; " writes the same ;

Without remorse, or any blush of shame !

These writings circulate, *are widely read,*

And many blight, to Christian teaching bred.

So goes the times, by Culture thus *adorned,*

Of *pious* living none too well informed !

Where it will end, whose vision can perceive ?

How much the prospect should all *thinkers* grieve !

Since natural law doth not oft make for *right,*

But fosters wrong from tyranny of might !

When *Scripture* fails to work its truths on man,

And he exclaims, " Believe it, ye who can ; "

Then lives as though no such a Word there is,

The saddest fate must come to him and his !

The punishment is *sure* for who *deny*

Their Lord and Master, and his truth defy.

Their fall, like *Lucifer*, will be so low

And everlasting, they will cry, " Ah, woe!

Great woe is mine, yet, is there no relief;

Christ will not pardon us this sin in chief, —

Dread *blasphemy!* that deadliest of wrongs

To hell, and *hell alone*, of right belongs."

Such, drifting are, on *Culture's* vicious tide,

Far, far away, from where they should abide —

Fast by the oracles of God whose will

Therein is *clear*, while Nature baffles still !

Is it for *this* — this reckless unbelief,

This overwhelming, bitter, *constant* grief,

That mental training is so freely given

" To help us here, and on, if there 's a heaven?"

How blessed are any, or for heaven meet,

Who only learn what fosters *self-conceit !*

Who say " mankind have outgrown God in Christ ; "

That " truth alone in *Nature doth consist;* "

Who mostly live a *sensual, selfish life,*

Ready in courts a disputant to knife ;

Though just his cause, and worthy of success,

Yet, must he lose it — Law, the *wiliest* bless!

Oh, when will God the selfish human heart

Which *wit combines,* inspire to nobler part?

When shall the weak *securely* hold their own

Against all power, even to the throne?

That time is coming, it is drawing near;

Christ, as is promised, soon will reappear,

To judge the Devil, *and who favor him,*

Content to live the shameless pests of sin.

When He on earth shall reign, then will obtain

Justice for all who love His holy name.

Satan confined, the wretches of his sway

Will slink, as darkness from the light, away;

Millennial peace and joy will be for those

Who do not Christ, in any sense, oppose:

With Him in power, the sinful will not dare

To injure whom, the Saviour's love doth share.

Laugh you at *this?* ye demons in the flesh !

Whom God permits his servants to enmesh

By sorrows many, through your carnal minds

And much good fortune, which with strength com-

  bines, —

Laugh you at this, indeed?   Prepare to see

God's word fulfilled — at every line — of *thee.*

The *wicked,* it is writ, will *cursed* remain,

This life their portion, endless death their gain!

Think you, the glorious Christ will fail to give

Their due reward to those who disbelieve

In Him as Saviour, Prophet, Lord, and Friend?

Hath He not said how such *base* souls shall end?

Culture, indeed! — what wisdom should delight

The Son of God, denying Him his right?

What human wit, however grand its range,

May in the Word one single purpose change?

And if that wit be *dead in unbelief,*

What more can Christ accord, than deepest grief?

Better by far, if Culture *gives away*

The souls of those which are for vain display,

To doubt and disbelief in Holy Writ, —

Better by far these souls had ne'er been born,

Than on the rack of Christ's displeasure torn !

True wisdom is to firmly stand for Him,

And shun those studies which such light will *dim:*

They lead to thinking, that will profit naught, —

Confused, uncertain, ay, and *evil* thought ;

To doubts of God, of everything *unseen,*

To picturing all things, simply, as a dream ;

But, if by Christ we stand, as Master, *Friend,*

We know how life began, how it will end ;.

We know how we should live to peaceful die ;

How, on Christ's word, we ever may rely ;

We kindly think of every one who strives

On Holy Writ, to squarely base their lives ;

We seek to aid them hold the faith professed ;

To serve them when, by unkind fortune, pressed.

One Lord we have, a Master we revere,

Whose cause we *love*, and have at heart most near:

Such is a *brotherhood* worth all the fame

The learned in doubt, may gather, as a *name* —

Vast in the knowledge of the ways to draw

Many to science from God's written Law :

But, who may sneer, at Christian faith shall feel

No joy in *that*, but rather woe than weal.

From such we turn — how cultured they may be —

As Satan's own, averse, O Lord, to thee.

Yes, intellectual people ! who should raise

All social, business life, to Scripture praise,

In *numbers large* use all the means they can

To curse with *vanity* the creature, man! —

To set him up *above* where he should rise;

On Reason perched, disputing with the skies —

Believing, yet, he will out-measure all

Therein that's grand, which natural laws we call;

Though, ignorant still, of how these laws obtain, —

The simplest, even, puts his wit to shame!

Sad, sad it is, such numbers lead the way

To boastful Reason's stupid, godless sway!

This *bad* example tells upon the crowd,

Who, in their turn, of unbelief are proud;

Doubting of all the senses can't discern,

With Holy Writ they won't themselves concern.

Yet, could *these see*, in those who ever stand

High as to wit, and high, too, in command,

A tone and temper in accord with Christ,

The good example *few* would e'er resist.

Whom fortune places far above the mass,

Are watched by these, a most observing class;

And, as their leaders and their *patterns* go,

So will they follow — be it weal or woe!

Important much it is, whom God has given

Good wit and culture to prepare for heaven,

That they should not mistake their duty so,

In other ways than Christian paths to go —

Drawn off by vagaries, not unlike some dream,

To bide with those, who make *themselves* supreme;

Who, 'gainst the oracles of God, declare,

Upon Him waging an eternal war!

That is a culture false, which wrecks the faith

In Jesus Christ — his birth, his life and death;

Whate'er we know, we 've little learned, indeed,

If we know not, how much this Guide we need.

Wisdom from science may delight our pride ;

But peace, alone, the Saviour can provide, —

That moral certainty, He taught, as God ;

In whom we rise, triumphant from the sod.

AUTHORSHIP.

As once I sat beside a beauteous stream

Where poets came to idle and to dream,

Far from the city's hum, the city's crimes,

So manifold in these blasphemous times,

There walked one near of prepossessing air,

With dark prophetic eyes and flowing hair,

Whom well I knew, and beckoned to my side,

Where sat he down, to ease and I, allied.

Some pleasant chat we had. 'Twas then he chose

To speak of authorship and author's woes :

So I, well pleased, encouraged the discourse,

Which he began with earnestness and force :

"Of all the vile and dirty work that's done

Beneath the rays of yon all-glorious sun,

The pen and those who wield its ' magic power '

Excel in wickedness through every hour.

What I essay will be to clearly show

Wherein the blessing, and wherein the woe,

Which springs, alike, from labors of the quill

So many venture, and so few with *skill.*

When, in my youth, I looked upon this life,

And saw few friendships unassailed by strife,

I turned to those who through the pen would say

Such noble thoughts, I longed to be as *they;*

I longed to write, to live, to think for all;

To feel, in Truth, I had a special call, —

To plead for her, to champion all her ways,

And pass in joy the balance of my days.

Unto this cause I gave my mind and heart,

Hoping to play a noble champion's part:

' Naught low, or mean, or useless would I give

To feed the public that I, too, might live.

The sea of trash which surged within my view

Much did I loathe, and its base authors, too:

The soul of honor in the trust I bore,

This stench of wit I could not but abhor.

My spirit seemed to wing its flight to God,

And I would tread where only Right had trod !

I wrote what pleased me, what I thought was well,—

I struck for heaven, as opposed to hell.

Full of the spirit of an honest pride

In that sweet truth for which I could have died,

I sought the publishers to aid my cause ;

But they, enslaved by *self* and selfish laws,

Could not do much for ' authors little known,'

How well might be what from their brains had flown.

They said that ' they were full,' and sent me where

Some other pubs like fulness would declare:

My thoughts, ambition, hopes were naught to these

Nor cared they me in any sense to please.

I must a name acquire, then, they would say,

' Welcomed art thou, we like you much, you *pay;* '

But for that name they would not stir a peg,

E'en though I kissed their hand, or knew to beg.

I felt repulsed when I would do a good ;

It stirred my ire and it boiled my blood.

Despite, howe'er, the usage I received,

O'er which the sensitive are often grieved,

I quietly reviewed these *little* men ;

And smaller even seem they now than then.

" Yes, in my youth, while yet by fancy led

To think all fair whose writings fairly read,

I deemed that authorship was truth itself—

A mine of Pleasure's richest, purest pelf.

But ' distance lends enchantment to the view,

And robes the mountains in their azure hue ; '

It gives to Letters a deceptive smile,

And cloaks in beauty what, too oft, is vile.

Now, young no longer, and no longer blind,

I see all life with clear, unclouded mind ;

Knowing most teachers of mankind to be

As mean, vindictive, as we care to see ;

While those who publish that which *they* may

    write,

By practice sharp, to bitter thoughts incite ;

And these two forces, leagued in ' *Truth's* behalf,'

Oft lack the worth of some fat kicking calf.

Yet do the public, by these *angels* taught,

Rarely consider but the book that's bought;

If *it* is pleasing, all the wrong behind

Is quite unheeded by the reader's mind.

So has it been, so will it ever be,

While those who read continue not to see

The channels whence to them instruction flows —

The arts of publishers, the author's woes!

" Would readers, students, only nurse a pride

In having *Right* o'er authorship preside,

The souls which live to send their thoughts to them

Through publishers, might have more self-esteem;

I say, might have, because I am not sure

If every friend to genius, Letters, swore

To read no books which came not from a press,

Whence came not, also, wailings of distress, —

I am not sure, I say, that *this* would gain

For Justice more than couples with a name !

The *traders* who have drank from author's skull,

Since books were made, their costly wine in full,

Will ever strive, I fear, to drink so still —

With *them*'s the power, with *them*'s the wicked will !

Some think it right to do what they may please, —

An author's interest it is fair to squeeze ;

And, as he can't be circulated well

Without some publisher his worth to tell,

He must submit to what these sharpers do, —

Those who demur are ' the superior few ; '

He must submit to what, perchance, they win ;

Cheat or no cheat, they are of need to *him*.

Yet, are there publishers, whose sense of right

Is active ever, and their dealings straight;

They know an author has an author's pride,

And with all wits their profits fair divide.

Yet, it is true, O Letters, all supreme!

Honor oft blushes at the counter mien:

Conceived in fraud, and frequent born in shame,

What hast thou but a most unsavory name?

Thou teachest strangely what is love and truth,

To nurse the virtue which may be in youth,

While, in the mysteries that breed thy life,

There's little else than mean, disgusting strife!

So that, to write as one would write, and be

Uncurbed by those who'd not have genius free,

There oft should be unto the author's name

The means to print, *as he may nobly aim.*

A *curse* are they with moral sense so small

They'll print, no matter what, but make the call,

(E'en though the taste is bad as bad can be,)

To nurture sin and weaken, Virtue, thee.

Go through the bookstores, lay your hand about,

Pick up a book, and ten to one it's stout

In merest nothings, and the money paid

Is thrown away by boy, or man, or maid.

To making books there surely is no end;

While truth and sense are on their last defend.

Most men who publish are a worldly crew;

Will give you poison, if naught else will do;

Debauch your taste, lay waste your heart and mind,

And all for *money!* — this it is we find

The why and wherefore of the *trash* on sale,

Before which sights the bravest hearts will pale.

How can it be that those whom God has given

Inventive wit, which dares its flights to heaven,

Will prostitute its powers to get in print,

That sin may revel in its darksome tint, —

To please those publishers whose evil wants

Demean the pens, which that desired grants.

" There are who write what none could ever read

Without acquiring some goodly seed, —

Something to plant within their souls to bloom,

Dispelling somewhat of Life's shades and gloom ;

Yet, are they told, ' their writings will not go, —

That sales, if any, would be only slow : '

They should their minds and conscience trim to suit

The taste, the fancy, of some human brute ;

Or, write for those whose simpering, mincing ways

Forbid them books intelligent to praise;

But, love-sick twaddle and the passion's glow

Is what they favor, all they wish to know;

Some vicious Nana, or, a tale like this,

Is what will suit the master and the miss.

If there are those who love to spend their days

(Deemed to be geniuses) for *such* to praise,

I envy not the fame that's so acquired;

By *me* such praise could never be desired.

" Who dare in verse to cast the laws of things,

To tell of Nature and the forms she brings;

To picture forth the secrets of her fame,

Their perfect concord with the Christian name,

Yet sees such works, conceived with purpose high,

Which teaches how to live and how to die.

Neglected, as a labor for an age

When *trash* and *humbug* may not be the rage;

Obliged to wait till comes that welcomed day

When ' what is *sound*, to publish *then* will *pay;* '

Obliged to wait while jackdaws flap their wings,

And all cry out ' What lovely darling things ! ' —

May well express some sorrow deep to find

So given much, to trifling things, the mind.

Whose is the life which could be better spent,

Than on such works, on truths so needed bent?

What poet writes the nonsense of the heart,

Who should precedence take of *them* in Art?

They who aspire, through verse, to give to God

As real a presence as the green grass sod;

While shallow poets but rehash the song

Of love, and all its self-same stories long.

Well, these *can* wait, and if, perchance, they live

Beyond this life (as I will e'er believe),

Well will it please them from their spirit home,

To see on earth the time for *them* has come,

When men and women will their works desire

To read with care, as they to thought retire;

Which treat of matters that should pleasure all,

And from misuse of life each reader call:

Revealing truths, whence lasting interest flows,

Whence, *true* delight, because of what one *knows;*

Whence, oft misfortune, may assuage its grief,

And find in age or youth, to tears, relief

Through God in nature, which around us lies,

Whose beauty lights the earth and spans the skies."

So spoke the poet, sadness in his eyes

From deep emotion, feelings some despise, —

Those heartless worldlings who can never know

A poet's passions and a poet's woe.

He spoke and paused, and then began again ;

Thus ran his speech in clear and earnest strain :

" Once, on a time, I went for generous aid

To one who dealt in verse — a godless trade !

Through him and him alone my hope must be

Of getting readers for my poetry.

' The verse was clever, subject fresh and new,'

But from *my* pen the Muses would not do ;

' I had no fame,' enough were famous now,

Who wore the bays upon their saintly brow.

And so, this keeper of the keys in Art

Poetic, playing an exalted part,

With face so hairy, full, and round, and fair,

And step so light, and manners free from care ;

With speech so soft and gentle, one would say,

He rarely sought, or seemed to want his way —

This smooth-tongued beauty of a certain set,

Who think in verse *their genius* should be pet,

Said to me softly, yet unknown to fame,

' To print your works would be to us no gain ;

We have enough to do for those who write

For polished tastes, alone, and minds polite.'

But said I then, ' You will your imprint lend?'

' That, sir,' said Beauty, ' we do not extend

Beyond the works we rightly call *our own ;*

No sooner published than they well are known.'

'T was, now, I looked in Beauty's gentle eyes,

And saw them full of just such kind of lies.

I said no more, but went upon my way,

Smiling to think what *little things will pay.*

The public ran for *him*, because, his art

Of clever humbug seemed to touch its heart;

But, could it know him as he knew himself,

Or, as God saw him with his fame and pelf;

Or, as some knew him through their common sense,

'T would say, ' Thou whited sepulchre. Oh, hence!

Out of my sight that other sights than thee

May come to comfort and to solace me.'

How *such* a fellow could position gain,

Which gives the bit to genius and the rein;

Commands the friendship of that brilliant mind,

Who painted Nature with a heart so kind;

Whose novels sparkle with deific power,

In characters we meet through every hour —

How such as *he* — a soul all dead to truth

Except what served him and his own, forsooth —

Could get and *keep* the place that he doth fill,

Is not explained — it is a puzzler still.

But oft it happens in the ways of life,

A harlot passes for a virtuous wife ;

Through art, by art, these wonders are attained ;

And so, by art this fellow got a name.

Well, let him keep it ; in those realms beyond,

Whence he has gone, and all of us are bound,

There shall he stand, *unmasked, a little* thing,

To whom so many would sweet offerings bring.

" When, in my youth, and rosy seemed my way,

And authorship a pleasure that would pay,

I plumed my wing to soar with Truth alone,

My conscience ever healthy in its tone,

Oh, how I revelled in that bliss so sweet,

Which waits on Ignorance's misguiding feet!

But abject quillmen of time-serving wit,

For dirty jobs in Letters only fit,

Have stayed my dreaming and its pleasures sweet —

Authors now seem the *meanest* men I meet.

A few there are whose virtues keep them true

To what, O Father! thou wouldst have them do;

But most who write for publishers and bread,

Alike to honor as to truth are dead!

As clay, within the potter's hand, they yield;

Assume such shapes adapted to *their field*,

And to the Shylocks of the paying press,

Who, wanton-like, love artifice in dress.

All hail! ye trimmers of an art divine,

Who prize so highly works you claim as thine;

Yes, *thine alone*, not borrowed or *purloined;*

But from your brain by honest method coined, —

All hail! I say, so dove-tailed and secure,

So sweetly winning and so saintly pure —

Your compact is a thing so shorn of *man*,

Let those fall down and worship you who can;

There are who will not praise what they despise,

Though others may the same thing dearly prize,

And read the nonsense you combine to print

In folios countless, with no wish to stint;

But would you stint in *this*, yet, liberal where

A generous act would make some life more fair,

That they could praise, and much admire, too;

That they could credit, cheerfully, to you.

But, say, O Authors! ye of fair renown,

Brimful of nonsense from your feet to crown;

Oh, say, if those who run the press through thee

Seem to delight in paying you your fee:

Do they not cheat you when the chance is theirs?

Are they much mindful of your pressing cares?

Would they a tear drop o'er your pleading grave,

When there you lay, a broken-hearted brave —

' Knight of the quill,' who drove it them to please.

To give them capital and much of ease?

If tears they shed, 't would be that no more thou

Could at their bidding make the ready bow,

And put thy wit in such desired dress

As would their coffers fill, their self-love bless:

Such crocodilic grief the gods behold

As wits reward in this vainglorious world.

The man of genius, if he wield the pen,

Too oft 's the sport of base designing men:

Had he the means to print, as he would write,

N'er subject to another's oversight,

There would to him be left a name to prize,

Worthy of love in his all-seeing eyes.

But, as the trade goes on like any trade,

And books for *money* mostly now are made,

The crowd of authors will their stomachs fill,

E'en at the cost of flooding earth with ill;

Their conscience is a thing of plastic kind;

So good or evil streams from out their mind

As it may *pay*, or publishers *demand* —

Such writers take they freely by the hand.

Well, let them take; the devil knows his own,

And wits are devilish which to this have grown.

Yet, praised be God, some in the Pen delight

Who will not flourish by ignoring Right;

Nor seek to prosper by a pregnant knee,

Crooked but for thrift — a fat though Christless fee :

These do not take to dark, ignoble ways,

To money get by courting vulgar praise ;

They were not born to be the slaves of *sense*,

And sell their souls for shillings, pounds, or pence ;

They are the enemies to knaves and sin,

Nor plaudits loud by favoring *wrong* would win.

As goes the custom in this ' art divine,'

Money secures most any sort of line !

Which flatters *follies*, what is good strikes down,

Scornful of those who on such baseness frown.

·· I can but pity and despise the life

Which falls so readily beneath the strife

Of wrong with right, of shame with honor's pride,

And all for *name* on Fame's incoming tide.

Give me that soul, which, graced with rarest gifts,

Rises to God — to Him his creatures lifts ;

Spurning the pæans of a faithless crowd

Which for its favorites daily shout aloud —

That soul I love, that soul can trusted be ;

That soul, O Father, is beloved by thee !

That soul would authorship make sound and pure,

And as Sir Walter would not e'er endure

A word which, dying, it could wish to blot —

This was the standard of the pen of Scott ;

This is the standard which alone can give,

To high-toned genius any wish to live.

The literary sculpins then would cease ;

These graceless creatures no more could increase ;

And time not distant would behold them all

Extinguished fully, past, perhaps, recall.

Oh, haste that time, that happy time when trash

Will cease to please, or largely ' draw the cash ; '

When verse no longer shall mere *lies* convey,

To please the fancy, vulgar passions sway ;

When genius shall to truth be true as steel,

Though lightly loved, and scanty be its meal.

What 's worth the praise, what 's worth the curséd

    gold

Of those who buy you — to their purpose sold !

Teach them to know, you 'll write to make your mark

Only as conscience fans, Ambition's spark ;

That what you write shall be what *all* may read,

Nor lose their time, nor morals make to bleed.

The vain, time-serving Authors of the day,

But fool their own and other lives away.

If in the pulpit they may chance to be,

They 'll put, Jehovah, outrage near to Thee;

With no religion but the love of praise,

No work 's too dirty if 't will plaudits raise.

If goes this on, with it will go the right

Which Freedom snatched from out the grasp of
        Might;

The right to *govern self*, to be a *man;*

To think, to act, on one's own chosen plan.

A Press debauched by wits because it *pays*,

Must bring to speedy close these prosperous days.

Nations decay when genius won't aspire,

To check the people in each mean desire.

Where it unites with them in sordid life,

Comes havoc quickly on the wings of strife;

And throats are cut as pastime for a mob

Which gloats o'er blood, and laughs to hear the sob.

My heart is sad, my spirit chafes to see

What may proceed from authorship and thee,

When 'pens employed' write only of what *sells,*

Ignoring Conscience, which 'gainst this rebels."

Thus spoke the poet as his eyes flashed fire,

And lashed his soul by proud and honest ire.

He paused a moment, then went on to say

More of the subject in his former way :

"Wherein the blessing and wherein the woe

From quillmen's labors, I've proposed to show.

Blessed are those authors and those readers, too,

Whose books delight, yet never injure you.

There are not many of this class who gain

Distinguished honor in a world-wide fame ;

Yet, they who'll follow these and cheer them on,

Will keep those ways where love is surely won ;

Those ways of pleasantness, those paths of peace,

Where kindly thoughts and kindly acts increase;

Where the deep sorrows of an evil life

Are all unknown with its malignant strife.

Herein is blessed who reads a wit so given,

Who'd have us know, while yet on earth, of heaven;

Who'd plume our minds and hearts to mount to
          God,

To bear with patience his chastising rod;

Who'd have us prize the beautiful in all,

And at Truth's shrine in bending posture fall;

Who'd teach us how to live, and how to die;

To love our Maker, naught in Him decry,

E'en though with tears he floods our daily bread;

Yet, will such authors, by God's spirit led

Keep us to Him who chastens those he loves,

Yet ne'er forsakes his suffering, pleading doves.

This is that genius whose delightful power

Can bless with peace when saddest is the hour:

Go to its works, and from their fountains draw

That life of Truth which flows for rich and poor.

Such mind, in whatsoever art it lives,

More in the right than in the wrong believes;

And rarely can be led to waste its powers,

As on the desert air, the sweets of flowers.

If those have lived whose large, surprising wit,

Has run in ways for virtuous minds unfit, —

If such there are in authorship to-day,

Who public morals strive to waste away,

They are exceptions which we must deplore,

And strive to *lessen*, not increase the score.

The soul which feels its might and knows its **reach,**

Is seldom apt the false and vain to teach;

Its spirit, sympathetic with the true,

Creates such love of God, such love of you,

That when instruction it essays to give,

Truth and its beauties must conspicuous live

In all it writes for keenest public eye,

That it may peaceful be, and calmly die.

Herein the blessing is of those who rate

As Authors, Artists, and esteemed as great.

If they are faithful to the trust that's given

By will of high and holy watchful heaven,

They must secure a flattering praise of earth,

When steadfast seen to everlasting truth!

Such are the blessings which from Genius flow;

Now we will see what writers breed of woe.

" Impelled by vanity to fame achieve,

In speed to gain it, they alone believe ;

They sharply watch the currents of the time,

Where float the *public*, ever, Folly, thine ;

And with these currents they will drift along,

To each false taste and habit weave their song.

They do not, will not seek to these oppose ;

They 'll chickweed give, if undesired the rose ;

They 'll dose their readers with conceits so mean,

That nothing good, proceeds therefrom, nor clean.

They do not aim the twig to bend aright,

Hence, grows the tree unpleasant to the sight ;

Exhaling poison, as the upas, round, —

That moral poison which in books abound.

Yet, though an author does in fact no harm,

Is flat and witless, neither cold nor warm,

Vending such manuscript as may be read

To no advantage to the heart or head,

But taken in where brains are thought to lie,

There float about amusement to supply, —

If such the worthless fruit his pen may bear,

Useless his life with all its work and care!

The drayman or the bootblack far excel

Such public servants in the cause of well.

A highly polished boot, a loaded team,

Is something more than ecstasies, a dream.

We pay these workers, in return we gain

Substantial service, not a reading vain;

Theirs is a life more worthy to be praised

Than godless authors by ambition crazed;

And even genius, when it writes on call

What must good taste and pious minds appall:

All these stand forward willingly to say

By pen and ink whatever 's seen to *pay;*

Then to the press their ' taking wit' present —

The veriest twaddle Culture could invent.

But what surprises most is how they live

Upon the public, they such nonsense give :

Yet, when 'tis seen what far too often draws,

And that ' the drama's patrons make its laws,'

Should it surprise us much that authors thrive

With marked success in keeping *trash* alive?

This is a sorrow no one will deny ;

All feel its pressure, some from it would fly ;

Yet, habit is all potent through the world,

Among the young, the middle age, the old ;

If used to authorship that points not high,

These lose the relish for a better tie.

So, wallowing in the mire of reading much,

While learning little from the pens of *such*,

Their lives in error drag of every kind,

By courting authors of ungodly mind,

Rather than those who are to conscience bound,

Pure in their habits, in their teachings sound.

" The young of either sex will spend their dimes

On authors writing only for the times,

But with remorse pursuing all their days —

Hating these ' wretches ' once they loved to praise.

I 've seen the fairest faces, fairest forms,

The gentlest spirit which affection warms,

Given to reading what never should be writ,

To demons grow, for evil only fit !

Religion's sense, without which none can be

Trusted by any — from suspicion free —

Was lost to them by *books* which bid them do

Whate'er their passions lead them to pursue.

Imposing no restraints, these works so bad

May for a price in many stores be had;

The booksellers, the publishers, combine

A paying trade to drive in any line,

Which authors follow for their sin-cursed bread,

While vast the crowd by their conceits *misled.*

The pulpit sees the moral wrecks I see,

But powerless it is, and so will be,

To save these readers from those well-laid snares

The Atheist and Infidel prepares.

That ' solid piety ' the *gown* should plant

Within the soul — its great eternal want —

It fails of doing through scholastic pride,

So far from Christ, who for us humbly died.

Why does it not its teachings make ' to tell,'

And save to heaven what is lost in hell?

It fails in this, because so weak in *faith*,

Whilst running *dogmas* fairly out of breath.

Ah, would it but believe in its discourse,

In clean white neckties given oft with force;

Would it but second heartily who try

To live like honest men, and nobly die;

Would it inspire the trust that what is taught

Is really that the Holy Spirit wrought;

Yes, e'en the *trust ;* it might *some* souls reclaim,

Which reckless authorship has sunk in shame!

But failing, thus, in bringing these to God,

While glibly talking of His wrath and rod,

How can humanity, with Life's large load,

Which bears them down at every inch of road,

And heavier is in Christian circles found, —

How can they feel a sense of *love* profound?

How *can* they or, the ' unbelieving damned '

Who 'll not *play* Christian — by too many shammed —

How can these minds, I say, get much relief

By airy doctrines merely of belief ?

Let but the *pulpit* and the *heart* conform

To that sweet Christ who stilled the raging storm,

Persuade by *loving* deeds, *not talk alone,*

Religion thus would gain a higher tone —

In dress and manners, and in action true

To that professed, Jehovah, as from you.

The charm of love but give to what is pure

And Christian-like, — we then may hear no more

Against the Bible, as a heavenly guide,

The good man's solace and the good man's pride!

This is the volume which, *believed,* can raise

Authors and Authorship to worthier praise.

I have no patience with those trifling minds,

Which, in a fling, mean pleasure often finds;

False in Science, in Philosophy the same,

With no religion but the love of fame;

Proud of the bravo of a Skeptic's sneer;

Of God nor devil, nor of man, no fear —

Their hopes, their pleasures by this life are bound,

Because unconscious of a state beyond.

These are the readers of, who ' liberal write; '

Whose virtue's easy, and whose pen is spite;

Working against whatever Christian claim,

May be set up in Morals' holy name.

But conscience outraged by their wish to be

Without command, O blessed God from Thee! —

That they may live a life to evil given,

And mock conditions to the joys of heaven,

Will rise in awful majesty at last,

With stern reproaches for the errors past,

To strike them as John Wilmot felt its blow,

The Earl of Rochester — that man of woe;

Or, as have *millions* sneering in their strength,

Come to embrace the Christian faith at length.

So may it be, with those who now employ

Their every power, to this faith destroy;

Yet, all their wit, and all it may essay

Can't wipe this comfort from the world away;

Which *Addison* sustained, as friends stood by,

When, said he, see how those in Christ can die.

I say that books and Authors not in tune

With *Holy Writ* — this ever priceless boon —

Infest the earth with woes that ruin more

Than years could number, or than hands could score.

Then, is the duty plain, to clean the press;

To read no books which *curse*, but never bless!

A man of genius is a man of stealth,

If Morals fail, beneath his touch, in health;

And if the public know its interests true,

'T will bid such geniuses a long adieu.

"Now, have I spoken, how are blessed or cursed,

Those formed by *Letters* and in Authors versed;

Nor have I been, ambiguous, but plain,

Which suits not some whose ways are dark and vain.

The error of too many pens is this —

They'll tell a truth, as babes will give a kiss;

So delicate and weak they lay it on,

That little else than waste of time is won.

Truth is a force that needs a fearless soul

To give it play, that it may get *control*.

The silvery tongue which melts through music's
strains

The icy heart, where nothing warm obtains,

Is well enough, its work is done with grace,

Among the righteous we assign it place.

But there are pens which will not softly state

The errors loathed, and which they would abate :

What'er is mean and false, they 'll surely slay ;

Nor stop to ask, if strikes like this will *pay*.

Yet, these are few — who like them not can go

Fast in those ways which leadeth on to woe ;

But they will stand where safe, sure footing is,

To conscience true, the highest source of bliss !

Oft are they told when writing to be read,

' They should take care, how what they think is said ; '

Yet, care they nothing but for what they know,

Out of their hearts and earnest spirits flow.

If called hard names and pelted, too, with *sneers*

By lofty self-conceit, which coarse appears,

They grieve to see what manners e'en obtain

With those of *rank* in Culture's motley train ;

Creatures who've managed to acquire note,

And would all others with reluctance quote ;

Assured that they, and they *alone* should sway,

Not letters merely, but in every way !

One can but smile at culture such as this,

While tempted much the vulgar thing to hiss.

And now, my friend — and friend indeed thou art —

Ere yet I close, and sunset beams depart,

I'll say, think only Authors serve thee *well*,

Who have a conscience over that they sell;

Remember, Authorship's a noble Art,

The mind should strengthen, grace with truth the

heart;

If this it fails to do, Oh, strike it down!

And heaven will bless thee, will thy virtue crown."

So spoke the Poet; as he rose to go,

I said, " Do stay, nor leave a brother so;

For are we not akin to all that's pure,

To all that's worthy of the mind to store?

Discourse again; I think you've more to say;

Come, sit you down, and give your thoughts full

play."

The Poet yielded — thus, his verses ran,

Freely and clear, as when he first began;

' What do we see so far in Culture's fields,

Which to our hearts o'er much of pleasure yields?

Methinks there's more, far more to pain the sight

Than glad it with the happy sense of Right;

Methinks there's more, far more to have us say,

Fame's thorny path is much too mean a way.

There are who think that those to Science given,

Have here on earth, a foretaste sweet of heaven;

And that companionship with such must be

A near approach, belovéd God, to Thee.

In this, again, 't is distance that deceives,

And robes ball mountains in a dress of leaves;

Misleads those minds but little up in lore,

The famed in learning almost to adore.

But those who know them well, their ways so vain,

From *gushing* praise will labor to refrain ;

Their moral sense is often near to shred,

And cometh so in getting daily bread.

Thus, life is seen ; as others they must do ;

Talk science up e'en while deluding you.

As Doctors, Lawyers, other astute things

Whose stay on earth unnumbered curses brings ;

As Artisans, or what not, they contrive

Smart tricks and falsehoods through each day to

    drive ;

Science with them, is ' how to make a pile,'

By means we see, too often are most vile.

The more they know, the more they seem to try,

Their way through life by subtle shams to buy ;

They 'll figure so, that none but they can gain,

While those ' done ' by them, plead their woes in

    vain.

Go where you will, look where you may, you'll find

That science, mostly, adamants the mind.

Its sweet affections, and its native truth

(Which may have blessed the hours of playful youth)

Is chilled to death ; and subject to this guide,

It heartless floats along life's inky tide.

Get knowledge ? Yes ; that is the cry around ;

Be up in all things, in our ears resound ;

Invade the planets and the nebulæ,

Look into all things, see what you can see :

Deny that God exists ; say, Man's from Ape,

And give to morals any kind of shape ;

Learn but to doubt, though doubt not you may rise,

Far more than others to be noted wise ;

Let *shrewdness* mark each action of your life ;

In science's cause, engage in daily strife ;

Be prudent of thy gold, on friends impose,

In all their business stick your sapient nose ;

And you shall rank among those ' able minds,'

To whom sweet Nature, all her stores unbinds.

Delightful creatures !   Ah, what should we do

Without your wisdom and your ' *virtue*,' too ;

What would become of Holy Writ, who knows,

With you not by to stay its desperate foes ?

You do so much to favor Christian law,

To forward justice, and to aid the poor ;

Your scientific facts are so humane,

For inhumanity we look in vain.

Ye votaries of science learned therein,

So cleansed by knowledge from the love of sin,

Come, tell us who it is that panders so,

To hideous vice which clouds our world with woe?

Who, methods name, by which the laws are dodged,

And vicious wealth in sumptuous style is lodged?

Who does all this?   Whence spring the guards which

    save

Vice from the Law when it the Courts may brave?

Can it be science, that meek, honest thing,

To aid the wicked, plumes its heavenly wing?

Can it be science, that would stoop so low,

To plunge in error those who strive to know?

Can it be science, which a mother's milk

Would stay beneath the fine full flowering silk?

Can it be science, which would dye the hair,

Contrive deceptions with especial care?

Can it be science which, in myriad ways,

With follies blight man's swiftly gliding days?

Ah, yes, it is, and pity 't is, 't is *true*—

That this, fair Mistress may be said of *you*;

But, not alone dost thou in meanness deal;

For virtue oft, thou wilt exert thy zeal.

Some noble souls there are by thee inspired,

Whose love of truth is all to be desired;

Faithful to *it*, they live and die for Right,

And those fixed laws revealed by Nature's light;

They are the lives without which earth would be

Cursed with a deeper hate, sweet Christ, of Thee!

Would there were hosts of such to crush the sin

Which Knowledge breeds, to heartless triumphs win;

Then would our world believe much more in prayer,

And in a Father's love, a Father's care.

" As I wade through the wickedness of man,

And see him grasp at everything he can,

See him well dressed and fair to look upon,

By whom so much is meanly, basely won;

Ready to do *whatever work will pay,*

Lawful or not, through every passing day;

Know him in science to be taught aright,

And with a wit so sprightly and so bright;

Yet, find him given to deception, shams,

I think how much of human life he damns!

Learning is well, but *morals* do exceed

All we can learn of value to our need;

Culture, to bless, must honesty sustain;

Stoutly oppose whatever 's false and vain:

Schools are but hot-beds of incipient vice,

If honor there, is seen but shrewd device;

If minds are furnished with ideas to *sway*,

With but a pinch of morals for the day;

If 'getting on' is all for which they learn,

For which they sigh, for which they madly burn;

On, on, in school, ahead in business life,

Whetting their wit, as footpads do their knife,

That, in the conflict of the days to come,

Their stabs may tell — be sent directly home;

Whereas, 't is *virtue* then should have the rule,

But fails through weakness bred within the school:

Cradle of character to one and all,

As nurtured there, they either stand or fall;

As nurtured there, the being winged for flight,

Rises to naught but ever cheerful light,

Or, falls where darkness folds the spirit in —

Those dismal shadows of the demon, sin!

Then, Culture, if thou wouldst a blessing be,

Let *morals* go in firmest bond with thee."

Here ceased the Poet, and rose again ;

When, we together walked, where waved the grain,

With that sweet sympathy of mind with mind,

Which makes this life so vastly more than kind.

We strolled admiring all delightful views,

And quite forgot the city and its news :

Nature we loved, by her so oft surprised ;

Her beauties charmed, we ever dearly prized.

And now, dear reader, unto you I turn,

Whom I would have of " cultured folks " to learn:

You've heard the Poet and so, too, have I ;

You may his teachings for yourself apply.

Are you displeased because he's spoken true,

And holds things up thus naked to your view?

If so you feel, my pity you evoke,

Since you can't bear an honest artist's stroke;

Since you can't bear to see how *small* a part

Oft Culture plays, both in its mind and heart.

Well, well, I pity you, and hope with time,

You'll say — "He's right, he's right, the wrong is
      mine."

And when you see that he has spoken truth,

By it be guided, if in Age or Youth.

So live, that when you come to pass away,

Many there'll be who'd gladly have you stay;

So live, that God may in your life be seen,

Whose love will keep your inner self serene.

Perhaps there are, who may these verses read,

Will say the Poet stands too much in need

Of skill and polish, to enrapture *them*, —

And so his verse they will at once condemn.

But sneers and ridicule, who may escape,

Who would aright the public conscience shape?

Our Poet, 't is confessed, is " no great shakes,"

From rigid rules, away he sometimes breaks;

Nor is he what is called a " darling dear ; "

So sweet, so *very* sweet, all far and near

Flock to behold him, and to press his hand —

No, no, such homage he does not command;

None beg of him a lock of his brown hair;

None say they love him, even to despair;

None throw their arms about his neck and swoon;

Feast on his eyes from early morn till noon;

Yea,— dewy eve, when twinkling stars shine bright,

And then is heard "the kiss me, love — good night."

No, no, our Poet's not " the rage " at all ;

Few kiss, or care in love with him to fall ;

Still, he survives it, and will write things down,

Careless of praise, or who may at him frown.

The friend of Truth, he would have all delight

In doing wisely from the love of right :

And if his pen is not exceeding rich

In " fine conceits," for which the critics itch,

He could point numbers out they're wont to praise,

Whose rhyme nor reason never make " a craze ; "

But, so goes life ; some credit get for *naught*,

While others good work do, on credit short.

Now, from me start upon thy mission fair,

Ye thoughts so true, ye children of my care ;

Whatever fate may on thy flight attend,

The just and righteous will thy cause defend!

For it is holy, therefore should prevail;

Who may oppose, are given to assail

Whatever hath a goodly form and tone, —

They love the devil and his works, alone.

But all who stand for Christ, delight in Him,

And seek to lessen, not engender sin.

These verses to His honor have been writ,

Imperfect though the melody and wit;

But if there are, of " greater parts " who shine

Only in Art, as " beautiful, divine ;"

Whose *morals* have no glimmer of the true,

And God nor Christ embellish what they do,

But Satan, rather, to their minds and hearts,

Seems better suited to their lovely Arts,

Then, it is well, who've any power to give

To Truth and Virtue, that these loves may live,

Nor be crushed out by Evil's solid train,

To wield that power, though they wield in vain.

Nobler 't is to strike, however weak

The blow that 's given for the good we seek,

Than, moved by fear, a dumb, dead thing to stand,

Lest some should jest of Satan's cursed command,

To see a weakling hitting out for right,

Willing to fall if worsted in the fight.

No meaner things are there than those who sneer

At what they say — " No *artists* can revere ;

Because of glaring, painful faults they find,"

While, what is worthy, wholly 'scapes their mind.

Such critics ever are — each age has known

Their mean injustice and imperial frown.

Blown up with self-conceit, — mere bags of wind,

Not one in many have an honest mind ;

But lie in wait, to pester whomsoe'er,

May chance to need, good will and fostering care.

An *honest* critic with a noble soul

Is loved, revered, from e'en the pole to pole ;

But they are *rare ;* 't is oftener far we see

The false enthroned, and mean as they can be ;

Who will say nothing in the way of praise

Of any writing, be it prose or lays,

From any motive to be strictly just, —

The critic will of something else think first.

What that may be, to guess is nothing hard,

He would consider the idea — reward !

What may advantage him, that will appear

The thing to do, the unctious motive dear.

Well, be it so ; these verses which are sent

Among mankind, upon the *Right*, intent,

Are so well armed in *honesty* and *will*,

They fear no critics, nor from them no ill.

Rather to hearts than heads they make appeal,

And ask acceptance for their truth and zeal.

FINIS.

NOTE.

In these concluding lines of "Intellectual People," I have had something to say of critics; and perhaps by some I may be thought not as respectful towards them as I ought to be. Well, I wish to say for *some* critics I have no respect, whatever; their so-called criticisms are simply *blackguardism;* they are a disgrace to the exalted vocation of professional critic; and live by abusing authors and publishers into feeding them. They have brutally abused me; and now I propose to take them in hand and give them a good spanking.

There are writers who will wait on the good or bad pleasure of these "pitiful creatures," with an endless patience and subserviency; taking from them the cold shoulder or a kick, most resignedly and amiably; in the hope that by and by their patronage may be fully secured. To such an order of aspirants for literary fame I do not belong; and no critic can truthfully contradict me. If what from time to time I have offered the public "has not been the best of workmanship," so be it; 't was mine and mine alone; and I am solely responsible for it. I have neither begged, nor paid any critic, to say what I have written was better than it really is. I have left them free to notice my works, as might suit themselves; and some have noticed with a vengeance, as will be presently shown.

But what else can be expected of *such* "intellectual people," who are placed as literary critics on papers and periodicals; whose pay for the service consists, mostly, in what they can "dead beat" out of nervous, shaky authors and publishers, and anybody else who is trying to live by serving the public, and need favorable press-notices. They never, or rarely find fault with the works of authors, as they receive them for a notice, whose popularity is general, and whose ability as writers, is thoroughly established in the acceptance of the people; even though it would be no hard matter to point out in not a few passages, what is exceedingly flat and oftentimes ungrammatical, — without either rhyme or reason. Yet the critic

has nothing but words of praise for the works by such authors;
playing the toady to these bright morning and evening stars, and
the "brilliant circle" in which these august bodies revolve. But
when the works are to be noticed of the lesser lights in authorship,
who are struggling to become "something more than common"—
entrenched also in the hearts of the people — straightway the time-
serving and unprincipled critics, turn upon them their batteries of
ill-nature and abuse; and, if anything is left of them, it is not because the critic has failed to do his best to destroy them. Every fault
in their works is magnified; what is really creditable is not noticed;
and wherever a sneer may be given, or ridicule conceived of any
line or page, there it is poured out unsparingly with brutal instinct
and heartlessness, and in a perfect flood.

As a very good illustration of this class of *gentlemen* "having
charge of the literary department of papers," critics, forsooth, —
I would say, when I published in the fall of the year 1883 my work
of "The Lost Love, and Other Verse," 12mo., 428 pp., I sent to
the press in Boston and elsewhere copies of the work for notice;
and, in a few cases, I sent with the copy a note in these words: —

"*To the Editor of*, &c.

"I send you a copy of my work of 'The Lost Love and
Other Verse;' and if you find anything to commend in the volume,
would be grateful to you for a kindly word.

"Very Respectfully,   THE AUTHOR."

A copy of "The Lost Love," with a note substantially as the
above, was sent to the "Boston Post," and the following gentle-
manly magnanimous response appeared in said paper, under book
notices: "We have received a volume of alleged verse, entitled,
'The Lost Love,' by Wm. Adolphus Clark, who sends with it
a note expressing the hope that we may not find it wholly uninter-
esting. We have not. On the contrary, we have found it very
amusing. It is the most ridiculous mess of silly twaddle, un-
mitigated rot, and dreary drivel that we have ever seen; and a single
glance at the illustrations in the book is enough to make a man
think he has an acute attack of delirium tremens." So much for
that fine *gentleman* of the press. This, then, is the way my cour-

teous solicitation was met for a kindly word in favor of my book, if in any part there appeared ground for commendation. To say that the brutal fellow who wrote this notice should disturb the mind of any sensible author, would be wrongly said. The impression such coarse blackguardism gave me of the "critic" was, that he could be nothing but a low-bred nobody; and that if in my note there had been some money enclosed, I should have escaped his brutality, at least.

While I feel certain the Editor-in-Chief of the "Post," would not have permitted such a notice of my book, to have gone out from his sanctum under the circumstances — or, in fact, under any circumstances, — yet, unfortunately for the good name of his paper, he had presiding over its literary department a fellow not only of bad manners, but of bad heart — a thoroughpaced blackguard! — since none but such a character would have given such a response to my courteous note. If nothing could be found in the book honestly to praise, its condemnation would have, at least, marked the instincts and breeding of a gentleman, had a gentleman criticised it. Of all whom I have heard speak of that notice, there is not one but has said "it is unwarranted and unpardonable abuse, not fair criticism."

The name that was given to me, as the writer of the same, I had never heard of before in connection with Letters; and I said to myself, "Poor dog! let him bark and snap his teeth; what possible harm can he do me?" When he says, "The illustrations are enough to make a man think that he has an acute attack of delirium tremens," we suspect that he must have been in such a deplorable condition from delirium of some sort, when he penned that notice, as not to know it would harm nobody but himself. Very likely he was just from a tippling shop, where drinks are free to the press; for such wits live by their wits, and never calculate to pay for anything they can sponge out of another. It must be a free pass for them everywhere, on pain of their blackguardism, if denied. As evidence that this notice was most unjust and far away from the truth, I would state a number of pieces composing the volume had been published in the "Evening Transcript," and other Boston and New York papers, and got there not by favor, but by merit. The editors, in some instances, had no personal acquaintance with me, and could have had no desire to favor my offering, further than in their judgment the merit of the same warranted. If they had not rated me as a poet, they would have rejected in every case my offerings.

If I do not put the music, the fancy, the imagination, and the nonsense into my verse, which poets of the "highest order of minstrelsy" put into theirs, this is a pity and a fault, to be sure; but people who read my verse will have to stand it. I give them in the cause of sound moral truth, what I think they ought to read; but, if they won't be at the trouble to read my writings, they are at perfect liberty to let them alone. I shall not quarrel with them because of their neglect; not *I*. I can be at better business. And as to those scoundrelly *critics !* who abuse and insult me, because I am and always have been unwilling to make love to them, I would just here say, that they are not worth in my opinion the powder that would blow them out of existence. I care nothing either for their praise or blame ; but against their abuse, I protest. One of them notices "The Lost Love" in the Boston Commonwealth newspaper in the following generous and *tasty* manner. A *gentleman* of the press, be it remembered, is responsible for all this kindliness and generosity. Says he : "The Lost Love pretends to be a book of poetry ; but after wading through floods of the dreariest nonsense, we have failed to find a line of poetry in it. The author thinks himself a *satirist*, and so he tells us in the awkward English of his Preface. He says he writes from a sense of duty. This magnificent personage, William Adolphus Clark, would feign be silent, but must be true to the public and dose it with what he has to say. He appears to think an elaborate dedication is necessary to every poem, and so his book abounds in them. His dedication to ' *State St.*' is magniloquent ; and, after this flourish of trumpets, the reader turns over the page, and is confronted with the following sort of twaddle : —

> ' When Justice, heavenly maid, was young,
>   While yet in early Greece she sung,
>   The Passions oft to hear her law
>   Would throng around her open door ;
>   Exulting, trembling, etc.' "

These opening lines of " State St." seem to make the critic very unhappy, for he goes on to say: "This William Adolphus Clark, this 'neglected child of genius,' is guilty of the grossest impudence in appropriating lines from Collins' famous Ode, to support in the most unconnected manner his own ineffable nonsense." Thus wofully affected is this precious specimen of a literary gag, to whom the Ode of Collins is — *very* sacred. " Could anything," he asks, " be more audacious?" Yes, my very fine fellow, the travesty of Hamlet; and the setting you up on any paper as a critic, who ought to be set down as a jack-a-napes. Further, says the fellow: " What an exquisite ear has our sweet poet Adolphus, who rhymes "door" to "law," and "overmuch" to "untouched," "came" to "rain," "sweat" to "heat," "own" to "foam," "bah! ha!" to "her." This point reached in his review of my book, he stops to say it is time he should forbear, and I should say so, too. He remarks that he would not clog his readers' appetites with too many sweets. What a considerate jack-a-napes, to be sure! and yet such a *sweet meat* as *he*, is constantly being commended to their appetites through his office of blackguard and critic. But he cannot, it seems, resist the temptation to say a word as to the poem, " George Eliot's Grave," where it is written, —

> "And if she lived as she believed,
> Who ill should speak of her remains."

This, it would appear, " is calculated to make him cry, until he laughs, were it not so much better calculated to make him laugh, until he cries." Was there, I would ask, any thing ever written by one of the "*intellectual people*," quite so lubberly as this? " A passage so thrilling, puts him in mind," he tells us, — "forcibly of a clergyman out West, — not East, North or South, but in the traditional " out West " — the blockhead it seems has to go a long way off for a story — "who," continues he, " when once officiating at a funeral very gravely said, My friends, we will now unite in singing the hymn beginning — " Awake my soul and with the sun," as it was a very favorite hymn *with the remains*." Having fired this very brilliant piece of wit off at me, with the assistance of " out West," he appears to feel some better; and giggling, tells his readers, he had marked several passages for quotation of the like richly imaginative sort. But he thinks enough has been said to indicate the treat that is in store for anybody who may purchase and read this book, which Heaven grant no one may be so unwise as to do. With commendable prudence the author has duly copyrighted his volume, and it is published by the Poet himself."

After giving me all this spite, he subsides: he thinks he has run his reckless, dirty, and dastardly pen far enough into my sensibilities. Behind the much vaunted "privilege of the press" he skulks for safety; yet his hide is not worth the tanning, nor his scalp worth the taking — who would engage for either job? That any important department of a newspaper should be in the hands of such a blackguard, is to be deplored exceedingly; and it is puzzling to understand how such management can be made to *pay*. Here is a wretch, who makes a wanton, and unjustifiable assault upon me, as an author, because I have not seen fit to propitiate *his* good will, by some subserviency to his office of so-called *critic*, which I am not in the habit of practising, even with those who could do me far greater services than the most influential and soundest of critics — then how could I possibly pay court to this Commonwealth literary gag? Were I a citizen of that sort, I should, no doubt, have many more friends; but, I prefer to get along with less friends, and more self-respect, more manhood.

The stupid, disgusting balderdash, which has been hurled at me, so unsparingly, malignantly, and remorselessly, indicates a very wrong condition of morals and of manners in the direction from whence it came. It explains itself clearly, however; every one must see no better treatment was bargained and paid for, then what else had I to expect? It is hardly possible for one capable of getting up any sort of a book, be it in verse or prose, say a 12mo. 428 pages, without there being on some one page or other something worthy of compliment, though it be but slight: yet, this Boston Commonwealth scapegrace left his readers to suppose, I had written and published a volume of verse of which not one word of praise would be justifiable. Is it a matter of wonder then, that against such unjust and unkind treatment of the Press, I am roused to complaint.

The annals of Letters give us many sorrowful instances, where the envenomed fang of some brutal unprincipled reviewer, has "laid out" the brightest geniuses ere they had become strongly enough entrenched in public favor, to successfully meet and survive the terrible annoyance of unsparing ridicule, vilification, and abuse — putting, finally, their heels upon these reptiles and mashing them. We all know how deeply they planted their stings into the sensibilities of Byron, Pope, Addison, and others, who turned upon them with a power of self-defence and protection which saved them from being destroyed. But such capacity in authors to meet and overcome a pack of malignant critics is rare, indeed. In general the rule is, to try and not incur their hostility; but, if assailed to patiently bear the assaults and survive them, if possible. Happily for authorship, there are among the professional critics, always some who will insist that justice shall be done authors, and when it is seen that any one of them is being persecuted, and written down from the sheer love of cruelty, true to the instincts of manhood and humanity, these lovers of fair play do their very best to defend an author so misused, whom venomous sneak critics, and literary vermin, would disgust with their evil spirit and blackguardism, and finally destroy. For the honorable and high-toned members of the profession of Critic, I have nothing but kindly words and feelings; their notices of my publications have always been fair: and while they have pointed out what could have been better done, they have been courteous in their dispraise; and cordially have recognized whatever there was of merit to note. As *gentlemen*, critics truly, they do not forget in their ardor of attack upon whatever is faulty or reprehensible in an author, to be at the same time strictly *just*.

I might lay before the reader several more low-bred notices of "The Lost Love," but will simply say, none are more offensive than those named, while some are fully up to that standard, and others nearly so. But I would not omit allusion to a notice of myself by a correspondent of the "Boston Saturday Evening Gazette," of Nov. 15th, 1884, signing himself "*Franklin*." What Franklin he can mean I know not, but if he has adopted as his *incognito* the name of the great American Scientist and Statesman, Franklin, the sooner he drops it the better, taking in its stead some other disguise.   Here is what he published of me, as a memory of Latin School days: "There were two," says he, "would be bullies in my day; one was William Adolphus Clark, the cracked brain Poet, and author of Anisetus.   He was abusing some of the boys and *stealing* their marbles, when Haliburton stepped up and settled his hash in short order."

It will be observed here with what elegance this "Franklin" writes — "settled his hash in short order," — and to be found, too, in the columns of that sweet-scented sheet — the "Saturday Evening Gazette," which pretends to be exceedingly nice in the choice of its language and its friends.   But to continue with this fellow's slang: "Clark gave the boys their allies, as Haliburton said to him, "Don't let me see you do that again, or I will give you another taste of the pump, and put your head in chancery."   This was sufficient: Clark subsided."

Then he goes on to tell what he remembers of the other bully, one *Henry T. Davis;* or, would-be bully, as he designates him.

When my attention was called, by a friend, to what this vulgar and abusive correspondent had written of me, I must confess to some surprise, that anything just in that kind of style should appear in the "Gazette," claiming to be a very clean thing, and the leading literary *weak*-ly Journal of New England.   I should have missed all knowledge of this "personal," had not my attention been thus called to it; since, for a long time I have studiously avoided all contact with that paper, and have never looked into it, even for an advertisement.   It is altogether too much of a *weak*-ly, too "previous" for me; too, too, much of a *swagger*.   Its *wit* and personals have very much the same effect upon the mind that an emetic has on the stomach — it makes one *heave*.

As "Franklin" earnestly invites us to reminiscences, I would state the memory is vivid with me, that in those old Latin School days the character of this paper was so flimsy, that it was generally known as the "Chambermaid's Gazette;" and among us boys was rarely called by any other name; nor, according to my way of thinking, is it any less flimsy a publication now, than it was then. As it has a so-called Colonel for its Editor, it ought to be of some account; yet, I cannot, nor can very many others, see that it is. As I had been published in this paper, as a bully, cracked brain, and a thief, by one of its low flung correspondents, I wrote this *gallant* Colonel-editor, remonstrating against such abusive and unlawful treatment, mailing the same to him, and requesting, as a matter of simple justice, that he should publish what I sent him in my defence; but he was not man enough, nor Colonel enough to do so. One is led naturally to enquire what such a brave, and fair-minded fellow is, or was ever a Colonel of? and if he ever set a squadron in the field, or charged a blazing battery? And the response comes: "Ha! ha! he charge a blazing battery, or set a squadron in the field? no, no; his forte lies altogether in another way than in *such* military work; and that is, in securing and enjoying a military title without any risk of life or limb. There are plenty of such titled men splurging around, who would be titleless had it been necessary for them upon the bloody field of battle, to have won their distinction."

This response seemed to me so exactly true and proper; and so precisely in accord with my own observation of *titles;* that I at once accepted it, as the very thing to say.

In my defence, which was denied publication in the "Gazette," I said I was neither the author of "Anisetus, nor did I know of any such a work; nor did I think any one else knew. To my early works, I said I affixed the *nom de plume* of Anicetus not Anisetus and this was the whole matter. As for the story about my bullying boys and stealing their marbles, and getting pumped on for my conduct, followed by a threat of being pumped on again, if I dared repeat the offence, I said, this story was all a fiction, and I wanted somebody's word besides "Franklin's," before I would distrust my own memory as to those long by-gone days, and the point at issue. I said, I could remember nothing of the kind; and I did not believe any creditable person could. As to the charge made, that I am a cracked brain poet, I said that is a mere matter of opinion: and where there are so many *cranks* around in these "intellectual times," it is a question if they who charge crank upon others, are not themselves even more insane. Yet, though I had a right to be heard in answer to this libellous, vulgar, reckless correspondent, yet, no hearing was granted me, nor was my communication even acknowledged. And why? Because, had my reply to " Franklin " in full appeared in the " Gazette," it would have exhibited in so clear a light the meanness of all concerned in this godless, graceless, lying personal, it would have added nothing to its good name. Not being allowed to defend myself in the paper which assailed me, I asked the privilege of addressing " Franklin " in one of the leading papers; but the Editor said, " how could you suppose we would have anything to do with this dirty business of the Gazette." " Yes," I replied " it is indeed a dirty business enough, nor should I take any notice of it, but for the fact, that I don't like to be lied about, even by blackguards." " You should insist," said the Editor, " upon being heard in the paper that abused and libelled you; and failing, should fall back upon the courts. Now, as to being heard in the " Gazette," it was evident the *Colonel* did not intend that I should be, and I made up my mind not to press for the right; and as to the courts, whoever resorted to *them* with any such a case as mine, and obtained any satisfaction worth the trouble and expense of suit.

It, therefore, must be, if persons are insulted, libelled, and lied about by the "*gentlemen* of the Press," and they want satisfaction for the injury, they must get it out of these *gentlemen's* hides, or not get it at all, if only one's self-love is affected. But to get satisfaction out of such fellows' hides, is often to give them an advantage in law which the aggrieved party cannot always afford to do. In visiting with personal chastisement a blackguard and libeller, rogue and liar, the very satisfaction which is sought gives only, too often, the greater satisfaction to the mean contemptible wretch who is chastised. So that there seems to be no better way than to treat with silent contempt, people who have no more manhood than to play the sneak, the blackguard, libeller, and liar; and when they come in one's presence to turn from them promptly, as we should from those infected with the most loathsome disease. But should they become insufferably annoying, then, if the law will give to the sufferer no proper defence from the insufferable nuisance, nothing remains but for persons so annoyed, to protect and defend themselves by all the *man* there is in them.

I would not omit to state that I wrote to my old schoolfellow. Alfred F. Haliburton (when I had learned of his whereabouts), asking what he remembered as true of this story of " Franklin's," and he replied, he remembered only the circumstances, but could not recall to mind who the boy was he checked as a bully. Sure I am, that he never checked me. I think had *I* been the boy he put the indignity upon, as stated, he would have received in return for his rudeness such a Roland for an Oliver, that his recollection of *me* would be very distinct, as the boy who got the pump—he would neither have forgotten *my* person or *my* name. I was not in the habit in those days, any more than I am now, of allowing anybody to take unpardonable and indecent liberties with my person. And they who remember me as a boy, whatever their recollections may be of that long ago, will not, I feel very sure, charge that I was either a sneak, a bully, a coward, or a thief. If there are any such memories of me, they are by my enemies, who can, probably, always remember a good deal more than ever happened of those they dislike, whenever it suits their humor to do so. But it is indeed amusing to read this fellow " Franklin's " condemnation of the Latin School bullies, and tell-tales, and thieves of his day, when he himself is the meanest kind of a tell-tale and sneak bully; and, no doubt, if his record could be investigated, it would show him to have stolen, oft and again, things of more value than marbles, more priceless than rubies. He is the meanest kind of a tell-tale, inasmuch as he went to the public with stories discreditable to the characters of his schoolfellows, some of whom are not living to defend themselves, as I am defending myself against his calumny and fiction; and even if what he pretends to remember is in fact true, who but a low-spirited fellow would parade in the columns of a newspaper anything to the disparagement of one who was the companion of his boyhood, or merely a schoolmate? He is the meanest kind of a sneak bully, inasmuch as he strikes those who, dead, cannot strike back; or living, may from a prudential conservatism, fail to do so. He strikes, too, under a guise. Nobody knows, of whom I have inquired, who this sneak bully correspondent of the "Gazette" is. "Franklin" is something very indefinite. If he was ever christened, why does he not give us his identity. Such a beauty should not remain concealed. I have now done with those who have had to do with me, misrepresenting, vilifying, and insulting me in the most wanton and uncalled for manner; instigated, no doubt, in part by their mistresses — a class of creatures who have no reason whatever to admire some pages between the covers of "The Lost Love," which reflect upon the way they have of getting in with soft-headed swains, and keeping in until they have used them up, when they go on in their artful heartlessness and depravity, until death shall put an end to all further enterprise in "doing" soft heads and soft hearts.

Doubtless it will be thought and said by many, the more dignified and sensible course for me to have taken, would have been to have treated with silent contempt all these blackguards; but some, at least, who counsel thus do not know what the trouble, labor, and expense is of putting before the public a literary work, and the aggravation it is to the author, to have that public falsely told by so-called critics, whose book notices it is more or less influenced by, that said work is worthless and not worth attention. Could people in general know of such experience, they would understand far better why it is, I take extreme delight in such a note to my present work as this, and why it is, that I would if I could, drive every one of these literary scoundrels and vampires out of every civilized community in which they dared show their heads.

"Intellectual people," indeed! Such culture is doing more harm than good the world over; and what reason I have to write, as I do of it, I trust in a measure has been made plain. I certainly could wish that an education might insure good morals, at least; sincere friendships, and the noblest efforts for social advancement; that "the gentlemen of the Press" might be truly gentlemen, who would suffer no abuse of citizens in their papers; and when injury is done any one by an assault therein, give them willingly a chance to reply to assailants. I could further wish the religion of Christ might be made the foundation of all social and business life, and that mankind would deal kindly and honorably by each other; I could wish that Law, its character, administration and practice, might be made a blessing instead of a crying evil, and too often an absolute curse, to citizens. I could and do heartily wish all this for the best good of my fellow man; but how unpromising the prospect, that a *true* manhood and womanhood, will ever govern the world, and the intercourse of mankind, before Christ shall come again and the Holy Land, redeemed from its desolation, shall blossom as the rose.

Surely, the cultured classes should be able to answer the question, when will "Intellectual People" show themselves to be any especial improvement, as to human nature, over those who are not classed as "intellectual?" But, instead of being able to answer it, they simply smile incredulously at any suggestion, even, that the most complete development of the human intellect, can in itself establish, a happy condition of life in any of the grades of mankind. Some of them, certainly, have sense enough to know, that the Scriptures and their teaching, which are the oracles of God, alone can do that, as a *sincere* faith; yet, they are witness, that this divine Word and assistance is being largely by Culture undervalued and ignored, as something *not proved* to be of "any more account as from God, than any other ancient writings." Where, then, are we drifting, and what is Culture, as a real spiritual and social blessing worth, if it does not produce more godly, amiable, and charming men and women, more just and generous because of what they know, — in a word, because of their "superior advantages."

If knowledge does not make lives more beautiful, high toned, honorable, and fascinating in every way, — more religious and helpful to the cause of Christ, and, consequently, the more worthy of Heaven, of what absolute advantage is culture (and the immense expenditure of money, time, and patience upon it) to the best moral and social good of mankind? In the judgment of the writer, if "a high order of education" gives, as its product, a large crop every year of irreverence and irreligion, atheism and infidelity, insufferable vanity, self-conceit, heartlessness, meanness, and hypocrisy 't is far better people should study and know less, and love and worship the divine in Scripture more.